THE ZACK FILES™

How I went from Bad to Verse

By Dan Greenburg

Illustrated by Jack E. Davis

BASALT REGIONAL LIBRARY
99 MIDLAND AVENUE
BASALT CO 81621-8305

GROSSET & DUNLAP • NEW YORK

For Judith, and for the real Zack,
with love—D.G.

I'd like to thank my editor
Jane O'Connor, who makes the process
of writing and revising so much fun,
and without whom
these books would not exist.

I also want to thank Jill Jarnow,
Emily Sollinger, and Tui Sutherland
for their terrific ideas.

Text copyright © 2000 by Dan Greenburg. Illustrations copyright © 2000 by Jack E. Davis.
All rights reserved. Published by Grosset & Dunlap, a division of Penguin Putnam Books
for Young Readers, New York. GROSSET & DUNLAP and THE ZACK FILES are trademarks
of Penguin Putnam Inc. Published simultaneously in Canada. Printed in the U.S.A.

Library of Congress Cataloging-in-Publication Data is available.

ISBN 0-448-42042-2   I J

Chapter 1

How much control do you have over your mouth? I mean, does your mouth pretty much say what you want it to? Or does it blabber out whatever *it* wants to?

I used to have pretty good control over *my* mouth till this one time I'm going to tell you about. But first, I guess I should tell you who I am and stuff.

My name is Zack. I'm ten-and-a-half, and I'm in the fifth grade at the Horace Hyde-White School for Boys. That's in New

York City. My folks are divorced, and I spend half my time with each of them.

In my English class we're writing poetry now. We're studying a poem by a guy named Joyce Kilmer. I don't know too many guys named Joyce, but my English teacher, Mr. Hoffman, swears Joyce Kilmer was a guy. Anyway, this guy wrote a poem about a tree. It starts:

"I think that I shall never see
A poem lovely as a tree..."

"What's the point of comparing poems to trees?" I asked Mr. Hoffman. "I don't get it. Trees are going to win, hands down. I mean, can you climb a poem? Can you get fruit off a poem? Can you stand under the shade of a poem on a hot summer day? You can't. I mean, I just don't get the point."

"It's clear Zack has some very strong feelings about trees," said Mr. Hoffman to the class. "Zack, I think *you* should write a poem about a tree. In fact, I think everyone in the class should. And to inspire us, let's go to Central Park and really study trees."

Everybody liked that idea, so off we went to Central Park. We lay down in the grass. Mr. Hoffman passed around a bag of Fritos. We stared up at the trees and tried to make up poems about them. It was a lot harder than I thought it would be. In fact, it was impossible.

"I can't do it," I said to Mr. Hoffman. "I can't even come up with a single rhyme."

"Zack, you haven't been here five minutes," said Mr. Hoffman. "Give it time."

"OK," I said, but I knew he was wrong.

Then something bit me on the butt. A mosquito or something. I smacked it. After a while, it started to itch. I began scratching it pretty hard. Mr. Hoffman saw me and frowned.

"Zack, what are you doing?" he asked.

I was about to answer him, when suddenly everything got kind of blurred.

"Sir, a bug just bit my butt," I said.

"I'd prefer you didn't use the word 'butt' in my class," said Mr. Hoffman.

Then things got even more blurred. And words I hadn't meant to say started walking out of my mouth. I said:

"What would you rather hear—
A word like 'rump' or 'rear'?"

"Either of those would be better," said Mr. Hoffman.

I didn't mean to answer, but I did.

"Perhaps you wouldn't mind,
If I called it a 'behind,'
Or, depending on their use,
A 'poop-deck' or 'caboose.'"

"Zack," said Mr. Hoffman, smiling. "You're rhyming! See? I knew you could do it."

I wanted to tell him I wasn't doing it

deliberately; that I couldn't do anything *but* rhyme now. Instead I said:

"My father's Uncle Manny
Calls a butt a 'fanny.'
My Aunt Sophie, who is tiny,
Calls my butt a 'heinie.'
Grandma Leah, who is pushy,
Calls my butt a 'tushy.'"

"Uh, very good, Zack," said Mr. Hoffman.

A couple of the guys nearby started giggling. Mr. Hoffman's smile had kind of frozen on his face. I didn't want to say anything else. But I started blabbering again:

"Our baker, who likes puns,
Sometimes calls it 'buns.'
I also know some geeks
Who call their butts their 'cheeks.'"

Mr. Hoffman's face had gotten cloudy.

"That is enough rhyming now," he said.

I certainly didn't want to talk in rhyme after that, but I just couldn't help it. I said:

"In England, though it's dumb,
They call a butt a 'bum.'
In France, where folks are merrier,
They call a butt a 'derriere.'
And last spring, I think on Easter,
I heard someone call it 'keester.'
But call it 'can' or 'bottom,'
It is clear that we've all got 'em."

The guys were laughing. Mr. Hoffman looked really mad.

"Zack," he said, "if you don't stop rhyming, I shall send you home."

I squeezed my jaws together so I couldn't blabber any more rhymes, but it was no use. I said:

"I meant no disrespect.
It's not what you'd expect.
I swear to you that I'm
Really trying not to rhyme."

Mr. Hoffman phoned my dad.

Chapter 2

By the time Dad came to the park to get me, I was really dizzy. Also, I was beginning to sweat like it was the middle of August. Which it wasn't. Dad felt my forehead.

"Zack, you're burning up," he said. "I think you have a fever."

I was feeling so weak by then, I couldn't even speak. Dad helped me into a cab, and we went directly to Dr. Kropotkin's office.

"Well, well, well," said Dr. Kropotkin. "Zack and his dad. It's always interesting when you come. How is your little friend from outer space with the two hearts?"

"Fine," said Dad.

"So what's the matter now?" asked Dr. Kropotkin. "Is Zack turning into a cat again?"

"No," said Dad.

"Since I can still see him, he must not be turning invisible again," said the doctor. "So what's the problem?"

"My teacher sent me home
Because I made a poem," I said weakly.

"Because you made a *poem*?" said Dr. Kropotkin. "Making poems is an art. I can't understand why you were punished for making a poem."

"I wouldn't have if I'd stopped—
I rhymed until I dropped," I said.

"Ah," said Dr. Kropotkin. "Well, that's different, if you couldn't stop. That's a different kettle of fish entirely."

"Have you ever heard of a condition like this before?" asked my dad.

Dr. Kropotkin didn't answer. Instead, he put his stethoscope in his ears and listened to my chest. Then he had me get undressed. When he saw my butt, he frowned.

"Hmmm," he said. "Tell me, Zack. Have you by any chance been bitten by a tick?"

"I thought it was mosquitoes,
I got bit while eating Fritos," I said.

The doctor nodded his head.

"Then that explains it," he said.

"What do you think he has?" asked my dad.

"Rhyme Disease," said Dr. Kropotkin.

"Rhyme Disease?" repeated my dad.

"You mean it's like a sneeze?
My rhyming's a disease?" I asked.

The doctor nodded.

"Is it serious?" Dad asked worriedly.

"No, not if we catch it early," said the

doctor. "I want Zack to go straight to bed. He should stay warm and drink lots of fluids. And by all means, avoid anything that rhymes—greeting cards, songs, especially rap music—anything of that sort. If he isn't feeling any better by tomorrow, I want you to bring him back here."

We went home in a cab. As soon as we got inside the apartment, Dad gave me dinner and then put me right to bed.

The next morning, as I started waking up, even before I opened my eyes, I knew something was terribly wrong. I couldn't feel the bed underneath me. And something was pressing lightly against my head.

Slowly I opened my eyes.

Oh no!

I was floating about eight feet above my bed, bobbing right up against the ceiling!

Chapter

3

My head was touching the light fixture in the middle of the ceiling.

"*Dad, Dad!*

It's really bad!" I yelled.

Dad came running into my room.

"Zack!" he said. "What are you doing on the ceiling?"

I said:

"*I dreamed I was eating baked cod.*

I awoke with a feeling quite odd.

I opened my peepers,

And said 'Jumpin' jeepers—
There's no bed under my bod!'"

"I can see that," said Dad. "But are you all right, Zack? How are you feeling?"

"You're asking me how am I feeling?
What I'm feeling is not so appealing.
I feel like a goon,
Or a helium balloon,
Just bobbing my head on the ceiling."

"OK, Zack," said Dad. "I'm going to get you down, son. Don't worry."

Dad reached way up, grabbed me by the foot, and pulled. I floated down to the bed. Then I bounced off the mattress and floated back up to the ceiling.

"OK," said Dad. "I think I know what we have to do. Once I have you down on the bed, I'll tie you in place."

"You're going to tie me up?
I'm not a little pup," I said.

"No, no, I know you're not a pup," said

Dad. "But once I get you down I have to keep you in one place."

Dad raced out of the bedroom. Then I heard him in the kitchen, banging cupboard doors open and closed. A minute later Dad came back. He was carrying rope, a dust cloth, and a light bulb.

"As long as you're up there," he said, "could you dust the top shelves and change that burned-out bulb?"

I groaned loudly.

"OK, OK," said Dad. "Maybe that's not such a good idea. Let's get you down now."

Dad pulled me gently down to the bed again. He tied my ankles to the bedposts.

"There we go," said Dad. But whatever was pulling me upwards was awfully strong. I slid out of the rope and floated up to the ceiling.

"OK, that wasn't such a good idea

either," said Dad. "Let's go back to the doctor."

He pulled me down and helped me change into my clothes. I held on to the bedposts to keep from floating upwards again.

When I was dressed, Dad made a little harness out of the rope and put it around my chest. He attached one end of the rope to the harness. The other end he held. Then, we carefully made our way outside.

We must have been a strange sight, a man walking with a floating boy on a leash. People on the street tried not to stare. But a little kid we passed thought we were the most interesting thing he'd ever seen.

"Mommy, why does that man have a floating boy?" he asked.

"I don't know, dear," she said. "It must have something to do with the Macy's Thanksgiving Day Parade."

Chapter 4

"So, Zack," said Dr. Kropotkin. "How are you feeling today, better or verse?" The doctor chuckled.

"Dr. Kropotkin," said Dad, "Zack's condition is not a joke."

"I know. I'm sorry," said the doctor. "But sometimes humor helps."

"Not this time," said Dad. "Zack's not only rhyming now, he can't even stay on the ground."

"I could say I always thought Zack had both feet on the ground. Or I could tell him to stand on his own two feet, but I won't," said the doctor.

"Good," said Dad. "Instead of making bad jokes, can you tell us why this is happening?"

The doctor scratched his head.

"Frankly," he said, "we don't get too many cases like this one. But if I had to take a guess, I'd say it was all this light verse that Zack's been spouting. The light verse is making him lighter. If we can get him to stop rhyming, I think we can stop him from floating."

"And how do you suggest we get him to stop rhyming?" Dad asked.

"One thing we could try is having him say words that can't be rhymed. Like 'orange.' That might short-circuit whatever it is that's making him rhyme."

"OK," said Dad, "Zack, just say the word 'orange' and see what happens."

I nodded. I tried to say 'orange,' but nothing happened. I tried again. No sound at all came out of my mouth. I shook my head.

"Maybe it worked," said the doctor. "Maybe he's cured."

"Zack, are you cured?" Dad asked.

"You ask if I've become
A guy who speaks in prose,
Instead of one who babbles verse
Till it's coming out his nose.
I hate to disappoint you on
So serious a matter,
But, unhappily, I must admit
I'm not the former but the latter."

Dr. Kropotkin sighed.

"All right," he said, "so it didn't work."

By the time we got outside it had become very windy. It was all Dad could do to hang on to the end of my leash. I sailed about eight feet in the air. I felt like a kite. The wind blew me all over the place. It was a weird feeling.

Then, as we were crossing Madison Avenue, a really strong gust took hold of me. It tore the leash out of Dad's hands and lifted me high in the air.

The wind blasted me to the top of a huge maple tree. I hung on to the branches for dear life. I was so high, I was scared to look down. I must have been thirty feet up!

"Zack, are you all right?" Dad shouted.

"How could I possibly be all right?

I am practically dying of fright!" I yelled back.

"Well, I'm going for help!" Dad shouted. "Hang in there!"

I peered down. I was as high up as a three-story building. Much too scary to climb down. I watched Dad run to the end of the block to a fire alarm call box. I saw him yank open its little door and pull the lever. In a few minutes, fire engines would come.

A big black bird hopped up to me on a nearby branch. It cocked its head as if to say, "What the heck are you doing in my tree?" I thought it wanted to be friends. But then it tried to peck at my eyes! I pulled away from it so fast, I almost lost my grip on the tree.

The wind was whining through the branches. The tree was swaying back and forth. You don't realize how far a tree bends in the wind unless you happen to be on top of it. Or unless you're a bird. Plus it was cold. I shivered as I waited for the fire trucks.

"How are you doing, Zack?" Dad shouted up to me.

I was about to answer when I heard the sirens. Then a fire engine, a chief's car, and a hook-and-ladder truck came tearing around the corner. Firemen in shiny black fire coats and helmets hopped off their rigs and began hooking hoses up to a red fire plug.

"Where's the fire?" I heard the fire chief ask Dad.

"Oh, there's no fire," I heard Dad explain. "I called you because Zack is stuck up in the top of that big maple tree there, and he can't get down."

"Cat up a tree!" yelled the chief. "Crank up the tower ladder!"

"Zack's not a cat," said Dad. "Zack is a boy!"

"Usually it's the *cats* that can't climb down," said the chief.

"Well, Zack's not a cat," Dad answered. "Although it's true he still hides under the coffee table when I vacuum."

"Excuse me?" said the fire chief.

"Oh, that's just a holdover from the time

he got scratched by a cat in the Temple of Dendur," Dad explained. "He did start turning into a cat—grew whiskers, started hissing at dogs, that type of thing. But it never went all the way. He's all over that now, in any case."

"Uh-huh. You sure this one's a boy?" asked the chief suspiciously.

"Pretty sure," said Dad.

The chief gave Dad a long look, then got his men to crank up the tower ladder. The ladder slowly rose to meet me, like a drawbridge over a river when a boat wants to get through. The ladder reached clear to the top of the tree. As soon as it got into position, a big fireman started climbing up it.

"Hang on there, kid," he called. "I'm coming to get you!"

The fireman was as big as an NFL linebacker. He grabbed me in one huge arm and lifted me onto the ladder.

"You're safe now, kid," he said. "Hey, what the heck were you doing up here at the top of a thirty-foot tree?"

"I hadn't planned on being here,
It was a huge surprise.
But I'm glad you rescued me before
That bird pecked out my eyes."

The fireman looked at me suspiciously.

"Why are you talking in rhyme?" he asked. "Is this some kind of a joke? Hey, wait a minute, was this a crank call?"

I shook my head.

"Oh gosh, no—holy smoke!
I swear it's not a joke.
I'm really, really grateful,
And I know this rhyming's hateful.
Though I can't express my thanks,
My dad and I aren't cranks."

"Is that so?" said the fireman. "Well, if you ask me, this whole thing is one big put-on. Next time, we'll leave you up here!"

Chapter 5

A small crowd of people had gathered to see me rescued.

When we got to the bottom of the ladder, the fireman handed me to my dad. The people clapped and cheered. Dad held on to me tightly.

"Thanks for saving him," said Dad.

"Yeah, right," said the fireman. "I suppose *you* speak in rhyme, too."

"Not at all," said Dad. "And Zack can't help rhyming. He has Rhyme Disease.

Floating seems to be one of the symptoms. That's how he landed in the top of that tree."

"You're kidding me," said the fireman.

"I'm absolutely serious," said Dad. "We've just come from the doctor's office."

"Gosh, the little guy was telling the truth. Sorry for doubting you, kid."

I smiled at the fireman. He jumped on his fire truck. It started its engines and all the fire vehicles pulled away.

A man in a dark blue suit and a light blue shirt walked up to us.

"Excuse me," said the man. "I couldn't help overhearing what you told that fireman. Are you saying your son actually floats?"

"Yes," said Dad, "he does."

Dad picked up some rocks. He starting filling up my pockets with them.

"These ought to weigh you down enough so you don't go flying up into another tree," Dad said.

"The reason I ask," said the man, "is because I work for Macy's department store. My name's McMasters. We'd sure be proud to have your son in our Thanksgiving Day Parade this year."

"Thanks very much, Mr. McMasters," said Dad, "but we're not interested."

"Why not?" asked Mr. McMasters. "We've got Snoopy. We've got Bullwinkle. We've got the Smurfs. Your son would be in pretty famous company."

"My son is not a helium-filled balloon," Dad said. "We're not interested."

"We're willing to pay," said Mr. McMasters.

"We're not interested," Dad repeated.

"Tell me what you usually charge for a parade," said Mr. McMasters. "We'll double it."

"We don't do parades," said Dad. "C'mon, Zack. Try walking."

I tried. When I walked, I looked like Frankenstein, but the rocks were heavy enough to keep me no more than an inch off the ground. The man from Macy's followed us.

"You don't have to give me an answer today," said Mr. McMasters. "Go home. Chew on it awhile with the kid. Kick it around. Sleep on it. Then call me in the morning."

"We don't need to chew on it, kick it around, sleep on it, stomp on it, or anything else," said Dad. "We're not interested."

"Don't say no too quickly," said Mr. McMasters. "This could be the start of something big. This could lead to lots of other things."

"Like what?" said Dad. "Being a junior Goodyear blimp at Yankee Stadium?"

"Just think it over," said Mr. McMasters. "I'll be in touch."

We looked around for a cab, but there weren't any in sight. Then Dad saw something that got him excited.

"C'mon, Zack," he said. He grabbed my arm and dragged me into a store. The sign on the door said "Aquanauts Dive Shop." It was full of scuba gear—stuff for diving underwater with oxygen tanks.

A suntanned guy in Bermuda shorts came up to us.

"What's up, dudes?" said the guy.

"We'd like to see a weight belt," said Dad.

The dude guy winked at us.

"Gotcha," he said. He handed Dad a belt made out of heavy lead weights.

"Do you have anything heavier?" Dad asked.

"Dude," said the dude guy. "With a set of oxygen tanks, this is all the weight you're ever gonna need."

"But we're not *using* oxygen tanks," said Dad.

"Get out of here," said the guy. "Then how are you planning to breathe underwater, dude—with a fifty-foot straw?"

"We aren't planning to use the weight belt underwater," said Dad. "We're planning to use it on land. It's to keep my son here from floating away. He's got Rhyme Disease."

The guy winked at us. He obviously thought we were putting him on.

"Right," he said.

Dad paid for the weight belt. Then he put it on me and I tried to walk. I felt like Frankenstein again, but I stayed on the ground. I clomped out of the store after Dad. I didn't think I was going to be able to walk very far. Dad flagged down a cab.

It took me about five minutes to get into it. Frankly, I couldn't see how this was any better than floating. The driver watched me like I was a species of animal he hadn't seen before.

"I'm sorry this is taking so long," said Dad.

"Take all the time you need, pal," said the driver. "I started the meter as soon as you flagged me. If you don't mind my saying so, kid, it'd be a heck of a lot easier if you took off that weight belt and took the rocks out of your pockets."

"Yes, but then he'd float away," said Dad.

"What's he got, Rhyme Disease?" asked the driver.

"Yes," said Dad. "How did you know?"

The driver shrugged.

"I've seen it before. I've seen everything. I had a guy in my cab once who had Rhyme Disease. Had all the symptoms—the rhyming, the floating, the works. He tried everything to get rid of it. Even went to the Mayo Clinic."

"The Mayo Clinic?" said Dad. "How did they treat him?"

"Pretty well," said the driver. "They were nice people."

"No, I meant what treatment did they use on his Rhyme Disease?"

"Oh. Well, first they read to him."

"They did? What did they read?"

"Real heavy serious books to make him stop floating and sink. *War and Peace. Moby Dick. A Tale of Two Cities.* Stuff like that."

"And did that make him sink?"

"Nah, it just made him depressed. Then they fed him nothing but mayonnaise for seven days."

"You're serious?"

"No, that was a joke. It was the *Mayo* Clinic—get it?"

The driver cracked himself up over that. He was still laughing when he dropped us off at our apartment building. I was getting kind of depressed, but not enough to make me stop floating.

I was beginning to worry that I'd never get over my Rhyme Disease. I'd have to go all through elementary school with it. And high school and college. I'd have to marry a woman who didn't mind her husband talking to her only in verse. And who didn't mind going for walks with him on a leash or wearing a diver's weight belt. Maybe I'd only be able to marry a woman who also had Rhyme Disease. Oh boy, was I depressed.

Dad phoned my best friend, Spencer, and asked him to come over. Spencer is the smartest kid in my class. Maybe the smartest in our whole school. Maybe he'd have an idea about how to solve my problem. Or if not, at least he might make me feel better.

Chapter 6

"Zack, I can't believe it," said Spencer. "You still can't speak in anything but verse."

"Although I can speak only verse,
That's not the extent of my curse.
For when I am rhyming,
I float and start climbing
The walls—Could it be any worse?"

"Oh, I'm sure it could be worse," said Spencer. "Hey, Zack. Take off your weight belt and show me the floating thing."

I took off my weight belt. Immediately, I started floating up to the ceiling.

"Wow!" said Spencer. "That's so cool. But I can see how it might get boring after awhile. OK, well, if light verse is what makes you float, then try thinking heavy thoughts. Think about the fact that in a few million years the sun is going to burn out. Then everything on earth will be one big block of ice."

I thought about that for a while. About the sun burning out. About how going to the beach wouldn't have much of a point anymore. About how all the companies that make sunglasses or sunscreen would go out of business. About how cold it would be, even in Florida and California. About what it would feel like to be frozen like a TV dinner. It was pretty depressing. But it didn't make me sink.

"OK," said Spencer. "Here's another

heavy thought. In a few million years the universe will start contracting. Everything is going to collapse inward till it's just one tiny speck of incredibly heavy matter."

I thought about that for a while, too. About everything getting squeezed together like people on the number 6 subway train in rush hour. Or like those cars in a junkyard that they squeeze till they're nothing but a little cube of rusty steel.

Nothing happened. I mean, I was really depressed by what Spencer said, but I didn't sink to the floor or anything.

Then a shocked expression came over Spencer's face. "Uh-oh," he said.

Just then Dad came into the room. He took one look at me and screamed.

"Zack, your skin is blue! What in the world happened?"

I looked at my hands. Dad was right. My skin had turned a weird blue color. I said:

"It is true that my hands are quite blue.
I guess that my face must be, too.
Not too many boys
Have skin that's turquoise—
I just hope I don't land in a zoo."

Dad reached up and grabbed my wrist. He took my pulse.

"Well, your pulse is normal, thank heavens," he said. "But how in the world did this happen?"

"It's my fault, sir," said Spencer. "I was trying to bring him down. I'm so sorry. I had no idea I'd give him the blues."

Spencer looked miserable. I tried to cheer him up:

"I have heard of folks getting the blues
But not from their head to their shoes.
This is really new turf—
Hey, I could be a Smurf!
Will I be on the ten o'clock news?"

"This is terrible," said Dad. "First, you're

rhyming. Then you're floating. Now you're turning blue. We've got to do something. Zack, I'm taking you back to Dr. Kropotkin."

I shook my head.

"Well, who else could we ask about this?" said Dad.

"You know who knows about weird stuff?" said Spencer. "Our science teacher, Mrs. Coleman-Levin. If anybody knows what to do, it's her."

"But school is closed for the day," said Dad. "And I don't think this should wait till tomorrow."

"We could go to her home," said Spencer. "Since it's an emergency, I don't think she'd mind."

"Well, I don't have her home address," said Dad. "And I doubt that she's listed in the telephone directory."

"Oh, we know where she lives," said Spencer.

"You've been there?" Dad asked.

"Uh, yes and no," said Spencer.

"Excuse me?"

Spencer looked at me. I shrugged, then nodded.

"Not in our bodies, but we've been there," said Spencer.

"What?"

"Remember that time I slept over and you couldn't wake us up the next morning?" said Spencer. "That's because we weren't in our bodies. We learned how to do out-of-body travel from a book, and we hadn't gotten back yet. We were at Mrs. Coleman-Levin's."

Dad frowned at me.

"Zack," he said, "from now on, if you're planning to stay out of your body all night, I wish you'd ask me first."

Chapter 7

As we were leaving the apartment, I tripped and fell. The catch on the weight belt broke and I couldn't put it on again. Dad put the harness on me, and when we got outside, I trailed ten feet above him in the air

"Well, hello there," said a familiar voice. "Had a chance to think about my offer?"

It was Mr. McMasters, the Macy's guy.

"We didn't have to think about it," said Dad. "I told you before. We don't do parades."

"Why don't we ask the young man?" said Mr. McMasters.

He looked up at me and noticed my color for the first time. He whistled.

"Hey, that's terrific," said Mr. McMasters. "Blue skin! You could be Little Boy Blue, or one of the Smurfs. What a great gimmick!"

"It's not a gimmick," said Dad, "it's a symptom. And we still don't do parades."

A cab passed, and Dad flagged it down. Dad reeled me in and I climbed into the cab. Spencer climbed in after me, and then Dad got in. Mr. McMasters put his elbow on the open window sill.

"OK, what's it going to take to put your kid into the Macy's Thanksgiving Day Parade?" he asked.

"Read my lips, McMasters," said Dad. *"It...is...not...going...to...happen."*

"Boy, your old man is tough," Mr. Mc-

Masters said to me. Then he turned to Spencer. "What about you, son? Want to be in the parade?"

"I don't float," said Spencer.

"We could pump you up with helium and see what happens," said Mr. McMasters.

"Didn't you hear him?" said Dad. "He said *no*!"

"OK, OK, OK! Whew! What a stubborn group!" said Mr. McMasters as the cab pulled away.

It was harder than we thought getting to Mrs. Coleman-Levin's. We didn't know the address. The only time Spencer and I had been there was out-of-body, and we were flying at the time, so we didn't recognize the route from street level. Then Spencer had an idea.

"Zack," he said. "I'll bet you'd recognize it from the air. Why don't you climb out the window and guide us from above."

"No way!" said the cab driver. "Nobody is climbing out of any window in *my* cab to do *anything*."

"But my son can recognize the route only from the air," said Dad.

"Oh?" said the driver. "Why's that?"

"Because the only other time he went this way he was, uh, flying," said Dad.

The cab driver stopped the cab and turned all the way around in his seat to look at us.

"You want to run that past me again?"

"I said, the only other time he went this way he was flying."

"Flying," said the cab driver. "Would that have been in a jetliner or a helicopter?"

"Neither one," said Dad.

"More like a hang-glider?" said the driver helpfully.

"More like an out-of-body experience," said Dad.

The driver waited to see if Dad was going to say anything else. There wasn't anything else to say.

"Look, chief," said the driver. "I don't care if your son was hanging from the talons of a giant Peruvian condor, he is not going out of the window of my cab to guide us, all right?"

"Why not?" asked Spencer.

"Why not?" said the driver. "I'll tell you why not. Because this is a licensed New York City taxicab. And one of the rules in the New York City Taxicab Drivers Official Rulebook says: 'No passenger shall climb outside the window of the vehicle and guide the driver from above the vehicle for any reason whatsoever.' That's why not."

"How about if I give you twenty bucks?" asked my dad.

"Oh, in that case, fine," said the driver.

Chapter 8

When we got to Mrs. Coleman-Levin's, she didn't seem at all surprised to see us. Even though I had blue skin and was bobbing on the ceiling of the hallway of her apartment on the end of my leash.

"I hope you didn't have any trouble finding the place," she said.

"No, not really," said Spencer.

"Well, come in and sit down."

I slid under the top of her doorway and pulled myself into her apartment. Dad and

Spencer followed. Mrs. Coleman-Levin pointed to a gigantic beanbag couch and Dad and Spencer sat down on it. Well, *in* it, actually. It swallowed up everything but their heads and shoulders.

"How about you, Zack?" asked Mrs. Coleman-Levin. "You comfy up there?"

You ask if I am comfy, and I guess your
  question's serious.

Well, I'm dizzy, dazed, depressed,
  defeated, and delirious.

I'm afraid that I've become some kind
  of idiotic poet.

To listen to me blabbering is boring, and
  I know it.

I wish that I were boating or canoeing
  or rock-climbing,

Instead of floating, blueing, and this
  nauseating rhyming.

I'd rather be in Albany or Brooklyn
  Heights or Yonkers.

But am I comfy? Sure. And I am also going bonkers."

"Interesting," said Mrs. Coleman-Levin. "Can I get you all something to drink? A riki-riki cocktail, perhaps?"

"What's a riki-riki cocktail?" Dad asked.

"It's the juice of freshly-pressed crickets over ice, with spicy ground pepper sprinkled on the top. It's quite tasty, really. Would you like to try one?"

"No thanks, we're good," said Dad.

"So," said Mrs. Coleman-Levin. "What can I do for you?"

"We thought you could help Zack with his problem," said Dad.

"That depends," said Mrs. Coleman-Levin. "What *is* Zack's problem?"

Dad looked surprised.

"He just told you: He speaks only in rhyme, he can't stay on the ground, and his skin has turned bright blue."

"Oh, I thought there might be something *besides* that," she said. "I take nothing for granted. Well, let me see. I suppose you've tried the usual remedies? Having him speak words like 'orange' that don't rhyme? Reading *War and Peace*? Telling him about the end of the universe? The sun burning out? The universe contracting? That sort of thing?"

"It was the universe stuff that *gave* him the blues," said Spencer.

"Yes, that's what often happens," said Mrs. Coleman-Levin. "The problem there is that you're treating the symptom—floating—and not the cause—rhyming."

"I see," said Spencer.

Mrs. Coleman-Levin wrinkled up her forehead in thought.

"You know," she said. "I do have one thing that might be worth a try."

"What's that?" Dad asked.

"Something left over from my softball-playing days," she said.

"You played softball?" Spencer asked.

"For the Greenwich Village Poets & Scientists," she said. "I played first base."

I couldn't believe my ears. Mrs. Coleman-Levin a softball player?

"Get out of here," said Spencer.

"You don't believe me?" she said.

Mrs. Coleman-Levin opened the hall closet, reached in, and pulled out a lime-green athletic jacket. In big yellow script on the back it said "Greenwich Village Poets & Scientists."

"You weren't kidding," said my dad.

"I never kid," said Mrs. Coleman-Levin. "Now then, this jacket is a very special jacket. It's re-versible."

"What's so great about that?" asked Spencer. "I have a reversible, too."

"I doubt that *your* reversible jacket is

like *my* re-versible jacket," she said. "On one side it's re-versible. It un-rhymes verse. On the other, it's *versible*. It automatically turns everything you say into verse. Let me show you. This side is versible..." She put her arms into the sleeves and pulled it on.

"...If you wear it on the side that's lime,
Everything you say will rhyme.
But wear it on the side that's yellow..."

She took it off, turned it inside out, and put it on again.

"...then nothing that you say will ever
   sound
Like anything even approaching a poem
   of any kind
Whatsoever."

"That's very impressive," said Dad. "What would happen if you put that jacket on Zack? On the re-versible side?"

"Let's find out," she said.

She took off her jacket and handed it

up, with the yellow side out. I slipped it on.

"Now, Zack, say something."

I cleared my throat.

"What should I say?" I asked.

"He didn't rhyme!" said my dad excitedly.

"True, but he's still floating in the air," said Spencer.

"And he's still that lovely shade of turquoise," said Mrs. Coleman-Levin. "Zack, I'd like you to try something for me. I would like you to repeat the first two lines of Joyce Kilmer's poem 'Trees': '*I think that I shall never see, a poem lovely as a tree.*' Can you do that for me?"

I nodded, cleared my throat, and said:

"*I think that I shall never see*
A poem lovely as a bush, a shrub, or
*   something leafy like that.*"

"It's working!" yelled my dad.

"But he's still blue and floating," said Spencer.

"OK, Zack," said Mrs. Coleman-Levin. "Pay attention. I would like you to say those two lines backwards. Can you do that?"

I tried hard to concentrate. Then I said:

"Tree...a...as...lovely...poem...a
See...never...shall...I...that...think...I"

The instant I said the last word, I fell heavily out of the air and landed on my butt.

"Ouch!" I cried.

"Hooray!" yelled Dad. "He isn't floating anymore!"

"Uh, but his skin is still blue," said Spencer. "He must still be depressed."

Everybody stared hard at me.

"Zack," said Mrs. Coleman-Levin. "Listen carefully. Nobody knows for sure that the sun will burn out or that the universe is contracting. If those things do happen, it won't be for millions of years. What's much more important is that you're a wonderful boy, with wonderful friends and family who

love you. Now, get happy immediately or I'll *really* give you something to be unhappy about."

I thought this over. I felt a huge weight lifting from my chest.

"He's not blue anymore!" Spencer shouted.

"You cured him!" yelled Dad. "How can we ever thank you?"

"There *is* a way," she said with a strange smile. "Assuming you're serious about thanking me, that is."

"Serious?" I said. "Of course. We're so grateful, we'll do anything you ask."

"Good," she said. "All I ask is that you open yourselves up to new experiences. All I ask is that you toast our victory with me by drinking some riki-riki cocktails."

Dad, Spencer, and I looked at each other. We couldn't say no. So we all had riki-riki cocktails. Don't even ask.

Chapter 9

There was good news and bad news about Mrs. Coleman-Levin's cure. The good news was that I was never able to rhyme again. The bad news was that I was never able to rhyme again.

Mr. Hoffman couldn't understand it. At first he was going to give me a failing grade in poetry writing. But then Mrs. Coleman-Levin had a little chat with him. He decided that he wasn't going to give me any grade in poetry writing at all.

Oh, Mr. Hoffman did take our class back to Central Park to look at trees. But this time I was fully protected against tick bites. I wore my thickest long pants, and I tied the bottoms of the legs around my ankles with rubber bands. I wore a shirt with long sleeves, and I tied the ends of the sleeves around my wrists with rubber bands. I wore gloves and boots.

I also borrowed Mrs. Coleman-Levin's softball jacket.

Just in case.

BASALT REGIONAL LIBRARY
99 MIDLAND AVENUE
BASALT CO 81621-8305

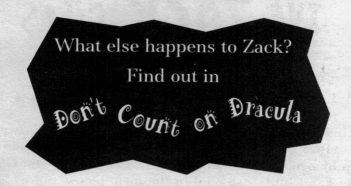

What else happens to Zack?
Find out in

Don't Count on Dracula

had to go through the Count's bedroom to get to the bathroom. I looked around. Hmm. Right opposite the bed was a mini-bar. I wondered if there could be any Dr. Peppers in there. I opened the door and looked inside.

No candy. No Dr. Pepper. All there was inside the mini-bar were about twenty cans of tomato juice. They were labeled "Type B Positive" and "Type A Negative." I took a closer look. Yikes! These were not cans of tomato juice. I was staring at twenty half pints of blood! I remembered the black candles and curtains and the black cloth over the mirror. Was Mella Bugosi a real vampire, like they said? If so, what were Spencer and I doing trapped in his hotel suite? And how could we get out of there before he decided to take a bite out of us?

THE ZACK FILES™

OUT-OF-THIS-WORLD FAN CLUB!

Looking for even more info on all the strange, otherworldly happenings going on in *The Zack Files*? Get the inside scoop by becoming a member of *The Zack Files* Out-Of-This-World Fan Club! Just send in the form below and we'll send you your *Zack Files* Out-Of-This-World Fan Club kit including an official fan club membership card, a really cool *Zack Files* magnet, and a newsletter featuring excerpts from Zack's upcoming paranormal adventures, supernatural news from around the world, puzzles, and more! And as a member you'll continue to receive the newsletter six times a year! The best part is—it's all free!

✂ --

☐ Yes! I want to check out *The Zack Files*
   Out-Of-This-World Fan Club!

name: _____ age: _____

address: _____

city/town: _____ state: _____ zip: _____

Send this form to: Penguin Putnam Books for
                        Young Readers
                        Mass Merchandise Marketing
                        Dept. ZACK
                        345 Hudson Street
                        New York, NY 10014